Feeling SHY!

Published in North America by Free Spirit Publishing Inc., Minneapolis, Minnesota, 2017

Library of Congress Cataloging-in-Publication Data
Names: Barnham, Kay, author. | Gordon, Mike, 1948 March 16– illustrator.
Title: Feeling shy! / written by Kay Barnham ; illustrated by Mike Gordon.
Description: Minneapolis, Minnesota : Free Spirit Publishing, [2017] | Series: Everyday feelings | Audience: Age: 5–9. |
    Includes bibliographical references.
Identifiers: LCCN 2017008396 | ISBN 9781631982569 (hardcover) | ISBN 1631982567 (hardcover) Subjects: LCSH:
    Bashfulness—Juvenile literature.
Classification: LCC BF575.B3 B37 2017 | DDC 155.4/18232—dc23 LC record available at https://lccn.loc.gov/2017008396

Free Spirit Publishing does not have control over or assume responsibility for author or third-party websites and their content.

Reading Level Grade 2; Interest Level Ages 5–9; Fountas & Pinnell Guided Reading Level L

10 9 8 7 6 5 4 3 2 1
Printed in China
H13660517

Free Spirit Publishing Inc.
6325 Sandburg Road, Suite 100
Minneapolis, MN 55427-3674
(612) 338-2068
help4kids@freespirit.com
www.freespirit.com

MIX
Paper from
responsible sources
FSC® C104740

First published in 2017 by Wayland, a division of Hachette Children's Books · London, UK, and Sydney, Australia
Text © Wayland 2017
Illustrations © Mike Gordon 2017

The rights of Kay Barnham to be identified as the author and Mike Gordon as the illustrator of this Work have been asserted in accordance with the Copyright, Designs and Patents Act, 1988.

Managing editor: Victoria Brooker
Creative design: Paul Cherrill

Feeling SHY!

Written by
Kay Barnham

Illustrated by
Mike Gordon

Fountaindale Public Library
Bolingbrook, IL
(630) 759-2102

ree spirit
PUBLISHING®

The new girl had been at school for three hours and she *still* hadn't said a word.

At recess, she stood in a corner of the playground and kept her eyes on her shoes.

Lily decided that it was
time to take action.

On Saturday, it was Olivia's birthday. Lily had been looking forward to her friend's party for weeks. It was going to be so much fun.

It was fun. They played musical chairs and Simon Says. Lily even won a prize!

But then she noticed that someone was *not* having a good time.

The next game was a three-legged race.
"Will you be my partner, Isaac?" asked Lily.
"If I have to," grumbled Isaac.

After a few minutes, Isaac was laughing as hard
as everyone else. He started talking to some
of the other children. And when he won a prize,
he wore the biggest smile at the party.

The next morning, Mom was
super busy cleaning the house,
while Dad cooked lunch.
"What's going on?" asked Lily,
dodging the vacuum cleaner.

"Did you forget that Auntie Pearl and Uncle Don are visiting?" gasped Mom. "Quick, go clean up your room. And tell your sister to do the same. I want the house to be *spotless*."

Auntie Pearl and Uncle Don arrived
in a flurry of hugs and kisses.
"Haven't you grown!" Auntie Pearl said
to Lily. "Er, yes," said Lily.

"So where's your little sister?"
boomed Uncle Don. "Has she grown, too?"
There was a squeak from behind the sofa.
"Come out, Violet!" said Mom. "Stop being silly."
But Violet didn't appear.

Lily crept behind the sofa.
"What's wrong?" she asked Violet.

"I feel shy," Violet murmured.
"If I come out, everyone will make a fuss."
"They'll make more of a fuss if
you keep hiding," Lily said.

"Hmm," said Violet, thinking for a moment.
"I suppose so." She took a deep breath.
"Surprise!" she said, bravely jumping up.
"There you are!" said Uncle Don.
"Haven't you grown!" added Auntie Pearl.
"Now, when's lunch? I'm starving."

The next week, Lily discovered for herself
what it was like to feel shy, when she visited
the badminton club for the very first time.

"Don't worry," said Dad, when he dropped her off. "You love badminton. It'll be great!"

Lily wasn't too sure about that. "Bye, Dad," she said, pushing open the door to the gym.

THWACK! THWACK! THWACK! THWACK!
Birdies flew back and forth.
Players leapt to and fro. All around, club
members talked and laughed.

Lily gulped. This was terrifying.
There were so many people here and she didn't
know *any* of them. What was she going to do?
She felt too shy to say a single word.

"IS EVERYTHING ALL RIGHT?"
bellowed a coach from the other end of the gym.
Suddenly, everyone was staring at Lily.
Oh dear. Now she felt shyer than ever.

Then Lily remembered how she'd helped others feel less shy. Hmm.

Could she follow her own advice ...?

Lily took a deep breath and went to speak to the coach. In a flash, she'd joined a game of badminton. And before she knew it, she'd made new friends.

Lily smiled as she whacked a birdie.
Feeling shy wasn't much fun. But making
friends was the best feeling in the world.

NOTES FOR PARENTS AND TEACHERS

The aim of this book is to help children think about their feelings in an enjoyable, interactive way. Encourage kids to have fun pointing out details in the illustrations, making sound effects, and role playing. Here are more ideas for getting the most out of the book:

★ Encourage children to talk about their own feelings, if they feel comfortable doing so, either while you are reading the book or afterward. Here are a few conversation prompts to try:

   · When are some times you feel shy? Why?

   · How do you stop feeling shy at those times?

   · When are times you feel really confident? Do you do things at these times that you could try doing when you feel shy?

   · This story talks about lots of situations where people might feel shy, such as going to a new school or having visitors. What other examples can you think of?

★ Have children make face masks showing shy expressions. Ask them to explain how these faces show shyness.

★ Put on a feelings play! Ask groups of children to act out the different scenarios in the book. The children could use their face masks to show when they are feeling shy in the play.

★ Have kids make colorful word clouds. They can start by writing the word *shy*, then add any related words they think of, such as *quiet* or *bashful*. Have children write their words using different colored pens, making the most important words the biggest and less important words smaller.

★ Tell kids that people who feel shy are sometimes called wallflowers, because they stand near the wall instead of joining in. Ask kids to draw pictures of themselves or someone they know feeling shy. Then have them draw pictures of the same person feeling more confident and outgoing.

★ Invite children to talk about the physical sensations that feeling shy can bring, and where in their bodies they feel shyness. Then discuss things we can do when we feel shy in a social situation, such as take a deep breath, smile, and stand up tall and strong.

★ As a group, brainstorm and practice things kids can say when they feel really shy, such as "Hi!" and "How are you today?" Even though these words and phrases are simple, practicing saying them out loud to other people can help kids use them in real-life situations. And these same phrases may help confident kids reach out to shyer children and help them feel welcome.

For even more ideas to use with this series, download the free Everyday Feelings Leader's Guide at www.freespirit.com/leader.

BOOKS TO SHARE

A Book of Feelings by Amanda McCardie, illustrated by Salvatore Rubbino (Walker, 2016)

F Is for Feelings by Goldie Millar and Lisa A. Berger, illustrated by Hazel Mitchell (Free Spirit Publishing, 2014)

The Great Big Book of Feelings by Mary Hoffman, illustrated by Ros Asquith (Frances Lincoln, 2016)

The Invisible Boy by Trudy Ludwig, illustrated by Patrice Barton (Knopf Books for Young Readers, 2013)

Two Shy Pandas by Julia Jarman, illustrated by Susan Varley (Andersen Press, 2013)

Willow's Whispers by Lana Button, illustrated by Tania Howells (Kids Can Press, 2014)